The use of too many questions has been avoided, as it is more important to encourage comment and discussion than to expect particular answers.

Care has been taken to retain sufficient realism in the illustrations and subject matter to enable a young child to have fun identifying objects, creatures and situations.

It is wise to remember that patience and understanding are very important, and that children do not all develop evenly or at the same rate. Parents should not be anxious if children do not give correct answers to those questions that are asked. With help, they will do so in their own time.

The brief notes at the back of this book will ...nts ...e

Ladybird Books Loughborough

compiled by Margaret West

illustrated by Robert Ayton and Martin Aitchison

cover design by Harry Wingfield

The publishers wish to acknowledge the assistance of the nursery school advisers who helped with the preparation of this book

talkabout

holidays

Planning a holiday

HOLIDAYS

MY TRAIN SET

What shall we take on holiday?

What is happening here?

Tell the story

L
YYB
746H
2
L
YYB
746H
4

Why have they stopped?

BROCKLEY HILL
CHELVEY MOOR

Which will you choose?

ORANGE
Sun
Spot

Talk about a railway station

2
3
29

Talk about the seaside

NEXT SHOW
2 O'CLOCK

Can you find your way to the castle?

Talk about travelling by air

Have you ever been on an aeroplane?

FASTEN SEATBELTS
NO SMOKING

Talk about a street in France

MARTINI
ALPHA
SI
CAFE
F

Tell the story

3
4

N
470

Have you ever seen one of these?

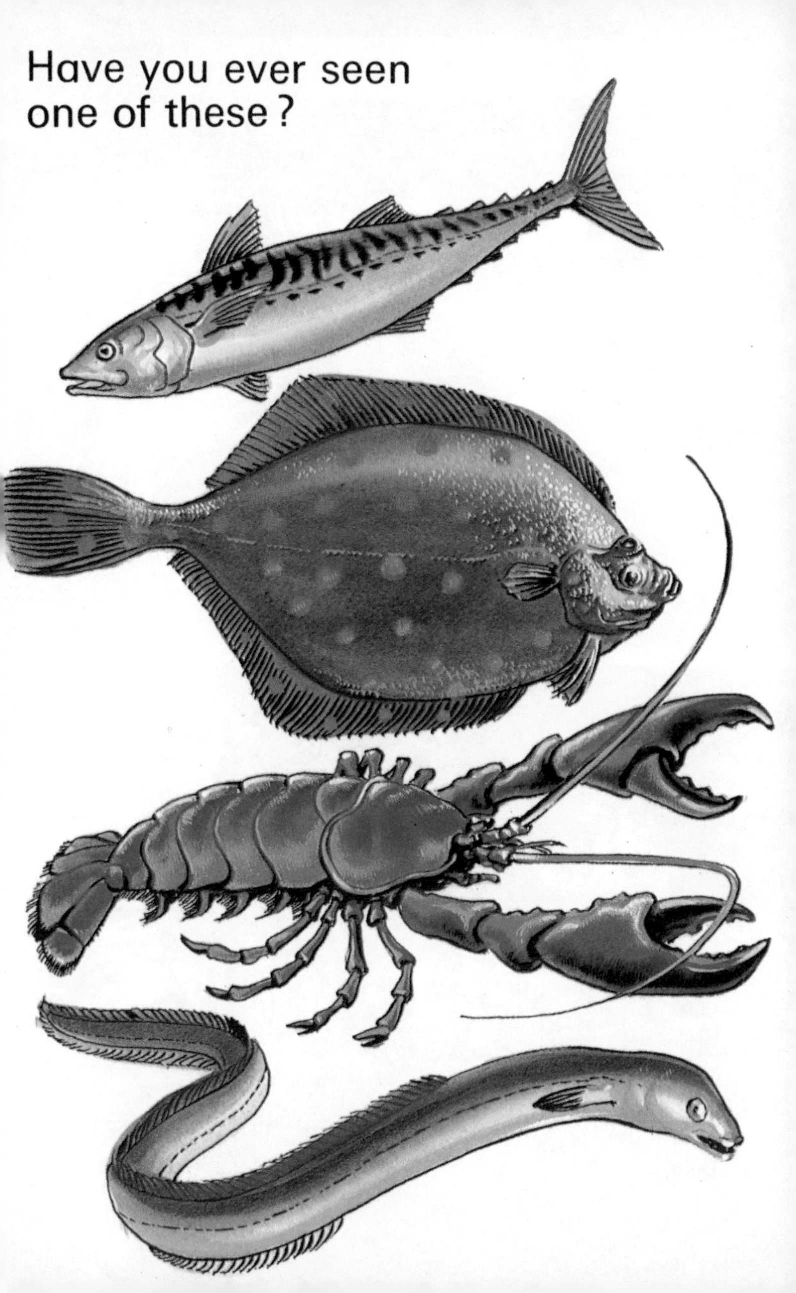

Things we enjoy on holiday

A holiday in the country

Can you find the lost kite?

DANGER
KEEP TO THE
FOOTPATH

Match each picture with its black shape

Talk about these famous London buildings

Houses of
Parliament
Clock
Tower

The
Post Office
Tower

Talk about these boats

. . . and the smallest?

Talk about a talent contest

Have you ever seen
any of these
in the country?

LOOK and find
another like this
and this
and this
and this

Talk about writing postcards

Goodbye to all the friends you have made

Suggestions for extending the use of this **talkabout** book . . .

The pictures and page headings in this book are only the starting point for conversation. Most children become excited at the mention of holidays and this interest can be encouraged and developed to increase vocabulary. Planning a holiday involves **choosing**; a place to go, a type of holiday, whether you go by **road** or **rail** or **air**. Packing brings in the question of volume and weight: how much will go into a suitcase, how much will it **weigh**, can you **carry** it?

Children love to make up their own stories from the picture clues, although they may need some help with the sequence to start with. Let them tell **you** the story. Will they take the cat with them? What if all the luggage doesn't fit into the car? Have you ever left anything on the roof?
What is a picnic?